Hot or Not?

Sam Carter

Illustrated by Dan Chernett

LONDON·SYDNEY

Gracias ('thanks' in Spanish!) to Jose Antonio who thinks I'm hot,
when sometimes I think I'm not! – TF

First published in 2009
by Franklin Watts

Text © Deborah Smith and Tina Freeth 2009
Illustrations © Dan Chernett 2009
Cover design by Peter Scoulding

Franklin Watts
338 Euston Road
London NW1 3BH

Franklin Watts Australia
Level 17/207 Kent Street
Sydney, NSW 2000

A CIP catalogue record for this book
is available from the British Library.

ISBN: 978 0 7496 9040 3

3 5 7 9 10 8 6 4 2

Printed in Great Britain

Franklin Watts is a division of Hachette Children's Books,
an Hachette UK company.
www.hachette.co.uk

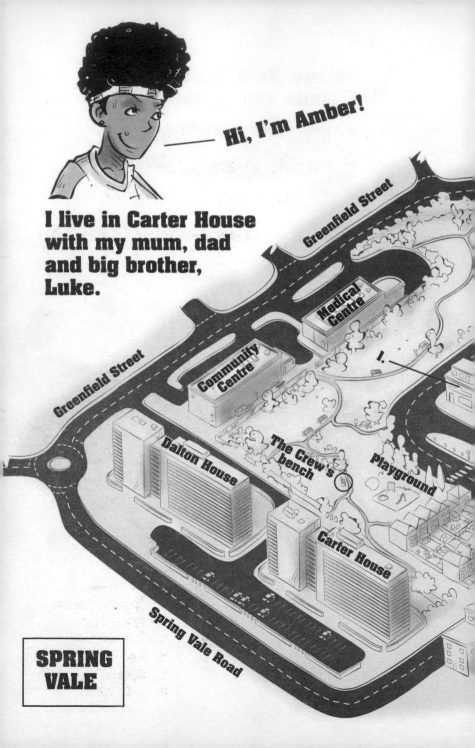

I love: sport

I hate: my brother's stinky feet

I want to be: a footballer or a games teacher

Best word: *GOAL!*

1. **Chicken House**
2. **Sleek Lady**
3. **Sun and Sea**
4. **Hot Wok**
5. **Empty shop unit**
6. **8 To Late**

Chapter One

Boy! My hair is really wild today.

I need an extra pair of hands!

I'm rubbish at all this girly stuff!

Oh, well – so what?

Time to meet the Crew.

I meet the Crew at our bench.

"Hey, Amber! What's with the big hair?"
Lewis calls.

"Do you want to borrow my hat?"
Harvey asks with a grin.

"Ha ha, very funny – not!" I yell.

"What's the fuss about?" asks Jade. "Big hair is in these days."

That makes me feel better.

Jade knows what she is on about. She always looks good.

"Is that Kai over there?" Jade asks.

I look over.

"Yeah, that's Kai," I say.

My insides feel all fuzzy!

Kai is so hot!

"Who's he with?" Lewis asks.

"That's Sasha from Dalton House," says Sam.

"She's well hot!" says Lewis.

Jade pulls a face at me. She knows I like Kai.

Oh no! They're coming this way.

I can't let Kai see my bad hair day!

"Harvey! Quick! Give me the hat!"
I say.

"So now you want it!" Harvey grins.

He holds it away from me.

I grab it and cover my wild hair.

Kai and Sasha walk by together.

We all stare at them.

When they've gone past, I take off the hat.

My hair springs up again.

How does Sasha get her hair to stay so slick?

The boys are still staring at Sasha.

"Man that Sasha is hot!" Harvey says.

"Really hot," says Sam.

"Mmm, very pretty," agrees Ravi.

So all the boys think Sasha is hot.

What about me?

Am I hot – or not?

Chapter Two

Next day, I'm in 8 to Late.

I'm waiting to pay for my football mag.

Sasha's in front with her mate Vicky.

"I told Kai it's over," says Sasha.

"How come?" Vicky asks.

"Just not my type, innit," Sasha says, as she pays for her stuff.

That's the best news!

Maybe I have a chance with Kai now.

But I'll need to look more like Sasha...

I run over to Jade's flat.

Her mum lets me in.

Jade's in her bedroom. She's painting her toe nails.

"Jade! You have to help me!" I say.

"How?" she asks.

"I need you to make me look girly," I tell her.

Jade looks up. "Why? You're fine as you are," she says.

I sit down on the bed.

"Kai's not with Sasha any more!"
I tell her.

"OK, now I see!" Jade says with
a grin.

She wiggles her toes and thinks.

"Do you *own* a skirt or a dress?"
she asks.

I hang my head. "No," I say.

I even wear trousers to school.

"Leave it to me," Jade says.

Jade comes to my flat with a massive bag of stuff.

She pulls out a short red dress.

"Er, where's the rest of it?" I joke.

Jade rolls her eyes. "You'll look hot in it!" she says.

"Yeah, but my legs are long and that dress is short!" I say.

Jade pulls out some black shorts.

"How about these too?" she asks.

"That's better," I say.

"Now for the make-up," she says.

She puts on eye shadow, blusher on my cheeks and gloss on my lips.

"Hair next," Jade says.

"OWWWW! That hurts!" I yelp.

She lets go – and my hair springs up again.

"No pain, no gain," Jade says firmly.

"OK, carry on then," I say sulkily.

It will be worth it to get Kai.

Jade grins – and brings out a big pot of hair paste.

Now my hair is slicked down like Sasha's.

Jade gives me a pair of girly shoes.

"Try these," she says. "Lucky we are the same size."

I kick off my trainers and take one of the shoes.

I try to push my foot inside.

"I can't get it on!" I yell.

Jade shakes her head. "Take off your sport socks!" she says.

"Oh, yeah," I say.

The shoes fit OK after all.

I look in the mirror.

Wow – is that really me?

"Let's go and meet the Crew," Jade says.

We see my big brother Luke on our way out.

I do a twirl. "Hey, Luke! What do you think?" I ask.

He looks up – and throws his snacks in the air.

"Legs…" he gasps. "My sister has legs!"

Jade giggles at his stupid joke.

Chapter Three

We meet the rest of the Crew at our bench.

"Who's your new friend?" Harvey asks Jade.

Me and Jade grin.

"It's me!" I tell them.

Their mouths drop open.

"Amber? No way!" Harvey yells.

"But, you look so..." begins Ravi.

"...like a girl!" ends Sam.

Lewis just stares.

Jade laughs and hugs me. "See!" she says.

The crew from Dalton House come over.

Denzil points to our football.

"You lot want a game?" he asks.

"Yeah, sure," Harvey agrees. "Six aside?"

I look at the muddy grass – then down at my shiny clean shoes.

"I'll sit out this match," I tell them.

Being on the bench is no fun!

I'm bored just watching.

It's a draw at one all.

"Watch Denzil! He's gonna score again!" I shout.

The Crew need me!

"Hang on! I'll be back soon!" I yell.

I rush back home. I'm gonna get my trainers!

I hurry back out with my trainers on.

That's better!

I put my girly shoes on the bench.

The Dalton House team had better watch out now!

"Amber!" Sam calls – and he chips the ball to me.

I dribble it down the field – past Denzil – and shoot.

"GOAL!!" the Crew yell.

YAAAAY! We won!

The Crew come over and hug me.

"Great goal!" says Marcus, one of the
Dalton House team.

"Mmm...thanks," I say.

But then I see Kai coming this way.

So I rush over and put on my girly
shoes.

This is my big chance!

Kai stares at me – and smiles.

My legs go weak!

"Hey, Amber," he says. "You look hot."

I shrug, to look cool. But really I can't speak!

"So, you wanna go out on Saturday?" Kai asks.

"OK," I say. Jade grins at me.

"Meet me at the arcade at two," Kai says as he walks off.

When he's gone I punch the air.

"Result!" I say to Jade.

Chapter Four

Saturday arrives. Today I'm meeting Kai!

Jade helps me out again.

She brings a skirt, a top – and killer heels!

I put them on and stand up.

"Try to walk in them," Jade says.

I take a step and begin to wobble.

"Jade!" I yell. I grab her arm.

"You'll get the hang of it," she grins.

I meet Kai at the arcade.

"I like your shoes," he says as we go in.

"Thanks," I say. But my feet really hurt!

A group of boys are in the arcade already. It's Kai's crew – they have come too!

They are playing a car race game – and Kai joins in.

I just stand there and watch.

It's so boring!

So I go over to play Dance Max.

My Dance Max score is rubbish. I can't move in this dress!

So I go back over to Kai and his mates. They are still playing.

They're going "Vrroom! Vrooooom!" like little kids.

And then Kai starts to pick his nose.

EEEUWW!

"Vrrooooom! Yes! I win!" Jason shouts.

At last! The game is over.

We all leave the arcade.

So far, my date with Kai isn't all that.

"The bus is coming!" Jason shouts.

We all get on and sit at the back.

Kai puts his arm around me.

OK, maybe he isn't so bad...

Then Marcus farts. Eeeuww!

"Bet no one can fart as loud as me!"
he says.

"Wanna bet?" says Kai.

Then he lets one go — only louder.

EEEUWW!

I push his arm away.

We get off the bus.

Kai buys chips from the Chicken House. Maybe he's not so bad.

We eat them on the swings in the park.

Kai chews with his mouth wide open.

EEEUWW! Again!

He burps, then throws the empty box onto the floor.

I pick it up and put it in the bin.

That's it! Kai is SO not hot!

"I have to go now," I say.

Kai shrugs. "Want to meet tomorrow?" he asks.

"No thanks," I tell him.

Kai stares at me. "How come?" he asks.

I think of what Sasha said.

"Just not my type, innit!" I say.

Kai walks off in a huff.

Ahhhhh, now I can take off these killer heels!

Next day, I meet the Crew.

"Hey, where's girly Amber?" Harvey asks.

"She's gone," I say. "It's the old me from now on!"

"Good!" says Lewis. "Girly Amber was weird!"

I pull a face at him.

"So? How did it go with Kai?" Jade asks me.

I hold up my hand. "It's over!" I say.

The crew from Dalton House come over for a game.

As we play, Kai walks past – with a new girly girl!

I look at Jade and shrug.

"Amber! It's your ball!" Harvey yells.

I run to meet the ball – and head it.

It flies past the goalie…

…and into the back of the net!

"GOAL!!" we all yell.

"Nice one, Amber!" calls Marcus from the Dalton House team.

"Thanks!" I say.

Now they have the ball.

"Marcus! It's yours!" one of them shouts.

Marcus takes the ball. He dribbles past Ravi and scores!

I run over. "Nice one, Marcus!" I say.

Then I take a really good look at him.

Mmm…

Come to think of it, Marcus really IS hot!

Car Wash

It's the first day of the school holiday.

I'm starved! And skint!

I walk past the Chicken House.

"Yo, kid!"

I look round. It's Zed, one of the
Cheetas, calling me.

The Cheetas are older than the Crew.

"Over here!" Zed says. So I walk
over to them.

"Yeah?" I say.

Zed hands me some notes.

"Go get us some food," he says.

"No problem, bro!" I say.

Cool! I'm down with the Cheetas!

Harvey cleans up at the car wash!

Harvey and the Crew set up a car wash. It's messy and fun — and it makes them some money. But then the Cheetas come calling. They want some of the cash, or else!

Available as ebooks from Autumn 2013

Catch up with all THE CREW adventures!

978 0 7496 9038 0

978 0 7496 9039 7

978 0 7496 9042 7

978 0 7496 9041 0

978 0 7496 9040 3

978 0 7496 9037 3